W9-CCI-804

I Can Read!

My First READING

Mittens

In memory of our cat Dickens
—L.M.S.

To Rob and Cyndi
—S.K.H.

No part of this publication may be reproduced, stored in a retrieval system, or transmitted in any form or by any means, electronic, mechanical, photocopying, recording, or otherwise, without written permission of the publisher. For information regarding permission, write to HarperCollins Children's Books, a division of HarperCollins Publishers, 1350 Avenue of the Americas, New York, NY 10019.

ISBN-13: 978-0-545-03795-2
ISBN-10: 0-545-03795-6

Text copyright © 2006 by Lola M. Schaefer.
Illustrations copyright © 2006 by Susan Kathleen Hartung. All rights reserved.
Published by Scholastic Inc., 557 Broadway, New York, NY 10012, by arrangement with HarperCollins Children's Books, a division of HarperCollins Publishers.
I Can Read Book® is a trademark of HarperCollins Publishers Inc. SCHOLASTIC and associated logos are trademarks and/or registered trademarks of Scholastic Inc.

12 11 10 9 8 7 6 5 4 3 2 1   7 8 9 10 11 12/0

Printed in the U.S.A.   23

First Scholastic printing, November 2007

I Can Read!

SHARED
My First
READING

Mittens

story by **Lola M. Schaefer**

pictures by **Susan Kathleen Hartung**

SCHOLASTIC INC.

New York Toronto London Auckland Sydney
Mexico City New Delhi Hong Kong Buenos Aires

Nick has a new kitten.

His name is Mittens.

"Mittens, this is
your new home," says Nick.

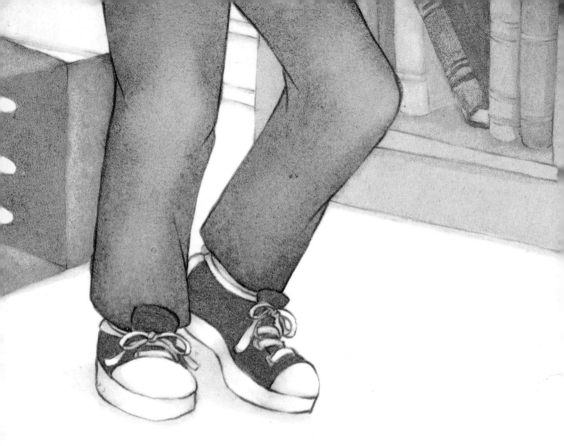

Mittens looks around.

Everything is new and big!

Mittens is scared.

Mittens wants a hiding place.

He wants a small place

just for him.

Zoom!

Mittens runs out of the room.

Zoom!

Mittens runs behind the T.V.

It is too loud.

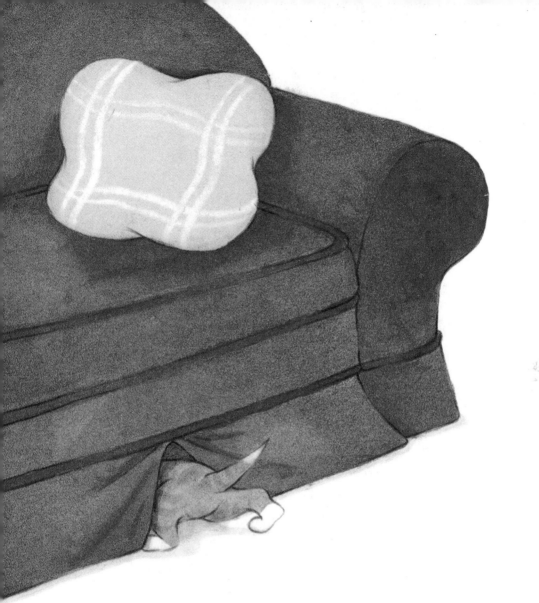

Zoom!

Mittens runs under the sofa.

It is too dark.

Zoom!

12

Mittens runs down the hall
and under a bed.

13

This is it!
Mittens has a hiding place.

14

He has a small place
just for him.

15

But everything is still new.

Mittens is still scared!

Mittens cries, "Meow!"

"Mittens, where are you?"
calls Nick.

"Meow! Meow! Meow!"

"There you are.
Don't cry, Mittens,"
says Nick.

19

Nick lies down.

"You are safe now," says Nick.

"I will take care of you."

Mittens moves toward Nick.
"I will be your friend,"
says Nick.

Mittens comes closer.

Nick waits.

Mittens curls up next to Nick.
"Welcome home, Mittens,"
says Nick.

Purrrrrr.

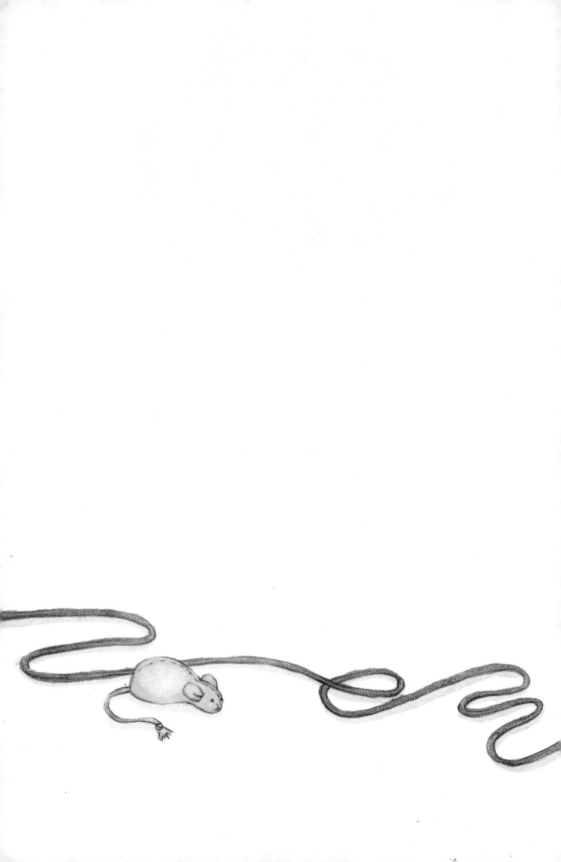